Contents

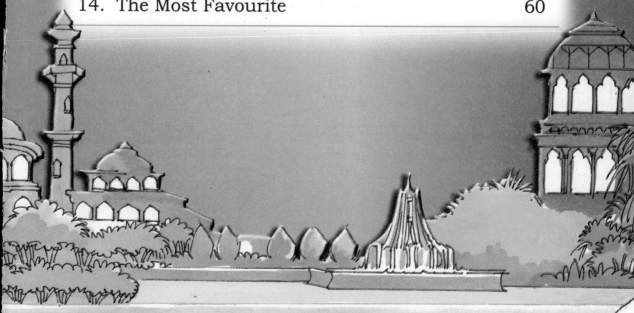

1. THE TEST OF A MASQUER

In the city of Delhi there lived a masquer. He used to entertain people with his shows in various disguises. One day, Emperor Akbar went to see his show. As usual, he was accompanied by his ministers and a retinue of servants. Everybody was engrossed in watching the show.

In the end, the masquer disguised himself as a bullock. Everybody cheered and applauded his art. Among the crowd of spectators was a young boy who was watching the show with great interest. Suddenly, he picked up a small pebble and threw it at the bullock. He was so delighted that, as a reward, he also threw his cap at the bullock. Emperor Akbar noticed the boy's act. He called the young boy to him.

"Young fellow, why did you throw your cap at the bullock?" asked the Emperor.

The boy replied, "Your Majesty, I gave the cap as a reward."

The Emperor thought that the young boy was a little mischievous. He said, "Reward? What reward? A dirty cap as a reward?"

With Love

To :

From :

Birbal, The wisE

Volume 1

Price : Rs. 95.00

NAVNEET PUBLICATIONS (INDIA) LIMITED

F1603

Preface

'Birbal' is synonymous with the rare and complex blend of wit and wisdom. Birbal stories are a part of our rich and varied tradition.

Generations after generations, readers immersed themselves in these stories. Going through the stories, a reader is exposed to varying experiences ranging from sheer humour to stunning revelations of wisdom. These stories usually take unpredictable twists and turns and spring up pleasant surprises at the end.

'Birbal, the Wise', is a collection of stories in two volumes. These stories provide recreation alongwith intellectual enrichment. These volumes will definitely prove to be one of those great and pleasant things that could ever happen to the young and impressionable mind of a child.

- The Publishers

 NAVNEET PUBLICATIONS (INDIA) LIMITED

Mumbai : Bhavani Shankar Road, Dadar, Mumbai–400 028. (Tel. 6662 6565 ● Fax : 6662 6470)

Visit us at : www.navneet.com ● e-mail : npil@navneet.com

Ahmadabad : Navneet House, Gurukul Road, Memnagar, Ahmadabad–380 052. (Tel. 6630 5000)

Bengalooru : Sri Balaji's, No. 12, 2nd Floor, 3rd Cross, Malleswaram, Next to Hotel Halli Mane, Bengalooru–560 003. (Tel. 2346 5740)

Chennai : 30, Shriram Nagar, North Street, Alwarpet, Chennai–600 018. (Tel. 2434 6404)

Delhi : 2E/23, Orion Plaza, 2nd & 3rd Flr., Jhandewalan Extn., New Delhi–110 055. (Tel. 2361 0170)

Hyderabad : Kalki Plaza, Plot No. 67, Door No. 6, Krishna Puri Colony, West Maredpalley, Secunderabad–500 026. (Tel. 2780 0146)

Kolkata : 1st Floor, 7, Suren Tagore Road, Kolkata–700 019. (Tel. 2460 4178)

Nagpur : 63, Opp. Shivaji Science College, Congress Nagar, Nagpur–440 012. (Tel. 242 1522)

Nashik : Dharmaraj Plaza, Old Gangapur Naka, Gangapur Road, Nashik–422 005. (Tel. 231 0627)

Navsari : 3/C, Arvind Nagar Society, Lunsikui Road, Navsari–396 445. (Tel. 244 186)

Patna : 205, 2nd Floor, Jagdamba Towers, Sahdeo Mahto Marg, Srikrishnapuri, Patna-800 001. (Tel. 254 0321)

Pune : Navneet Bhavan, 1302, Shukrawar Peth, Bajirao Road, Pune–411 002. (Tel. 2443 1007)

Surat : 1, Ground Floor, Shree Vallabh Complex, Kotwal Street, Nanpara, Surat–395 001. (Tel. 246 3927)

Vadodara : Near Hanuman Wadi, Sardar Bhuvan Khancho, Vadodara–390 001.

The young boy politely said, "Your Majesty, I appreciated the wonderful and perfect disguise of the masquer. I tested him by throwing a small pebble at the bullock. The skin of cattle is so sensitive that cattle shudder when it is touched by something. When the pebble hit the bullock's back, the masquer immediately shuddered. The masquer has passed my test."

The Emperor said, "But why did you give such a dirty and tattered cap as a reward?"

The boy said, "Your Majesty, it is more important to pass a true test. Whether the reward is a cap or a gold coin – it makes no difference at all. A gold coin given as a reward, without real appreciation, is not worth a penny."

Emperor Akbar realized that the boy was very clever. He took the boy along with him to his palace and employed him in his service.

This boy, after some years, became well known as Birbal.

2. A GREEN HORSE

One day, Akbar sat on his horse and rode into a garden. He was accompanied by Birbal. There were many green trees and lush green grass in the garden. Akbar was overjoyed to see such beautiful greenery. He said to himself, "What a pleasure it would be to ride a green horse in a garden like this!"

Akbar said, "Birbal, you must get a green horse for me within seven days. If you fail to get one, do not show me your face again."

A green horse! There can't be such a horse. Both Akbar and Birbal were aware of this fact. But Akbar just wanted to test Birbal's intelligence.

Birbal spent seven days moving here and there in the city under the pretext of searching for a green horse. On the eighth day, Birbal presented himself before Akbar. He said, "Your Majesty, I have found a green horse."

Akbar was surprised. He said, "Where is the green horse? You must show it to me right now."

Birbal said, "Your Majesty, it is a little difficult task. The owner of the green horse has laid down two conditions."

Akbar asked, "What are the two conditions?"

Birbal replied, "Your Majesty, the first condition is that you yourself will have to go to get the horse."

Agreeing to the condition, Akbar said, "Oh, that is very simple. I myself will go and get the horse. And what is the second condition?"

Birbal said, "Since the horse is of a unique colour, you will have to go and get it on a special day. The owner insists that Your Majesty must get it on a day other than the seven days of the week."

Akbar was speechless. He kept staring at Birbal's face. Birbal smiled and said, "Your Majesty, if you wish to own a green horse, you have to accept these two conditions."

Akbar was amused. He was pleased with Birbal's wisdom. Akbar realized that it was not easy to fool Birbal.

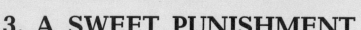

3. A SWEET PUNISHMENT

One day, as soon as Emperor Akbar came to his court, he looked at his courtiers and said, "Today somebody has pulled my beard. Tell me, what punishment should I give to that person?"

The courtiers were puzzled. They started discussing the matter among themselves. After some time, one of the courtiers said, "Your Majesty, the person who dared to pull your beard should be beheaded."

Another courtier suggested, "Who is that fool who dared to do such a thing? He should be trampled under the feet of an elephant."

Each courtier had a different suggestion to make. Akbar was bored to hear so many suggestions. Finally, he turned to Birbal and said, "Birbal, what do you have to say? How should I punish the one who pulled my beard?"

Birbal looked at Akbar and smilingly said, "Your Majesty, you should offer sweets to that person. This is the only punishment for this offence."

All the courtiers were baffled by Birbal's reply, but Akbar was very pleased to hear the suggestion. He said, "You are absolutely right, Birbal. But can you guess who could have pulled my beard?"

Birbal said, "Your Majesty, none but your darling little prince would dare to touch your beard. He must have done that lovingly! How can you punish him?"

Birbal was right. Early that morning, the Emperor was carrying his little prince in his arms. While playing, he had pulled Akbar's beard.

Akbar was very happy to hear the clever suggestion made by Birbal.

The rest of the courtiers were ashamed of their suggestions.

4. WHO IS THE GLUTTON?

Akbar was very fond of eating tasty food. He often threw banquets for his courtiers in the garden of his palace. Akbar used to enjoy a variety of delicious dishes along with his courtiers. And of course, Birbal's wit and humour added to the joyous atmosphere during the banquets.

Once, at one such banquet, Birbal was seated next to Akbar. After the meal, bowls of dates were served to all. Both Akbar and Birbal went on eating the dates and they threw the seeds under their chairs.

Soon there was a heap of date seeds under their chairs. Akbar saw the heaps and had an idea. He said to himself, "Let me make a fool of Birbal today." Quietly, Akbar pushed his heap of seeds under Birbal's chair with his foot. Birbal did not notice this act.

Suddenly, Akbar got up from his chair. With a surprised look on his face, he said loudly, "Oh! I cannot believe this! Birbal, how could you eat so many dates? I never knew that you were such a glutton!"

All the courtiers heard this and looked at the big heap of seeds under Birbal's chair. Birbal realized that Akbar had played a clever trick on him. But Birbal was equally clever. How could he allow the Emperor and the courtiers to ridicule him?

He immediately said to Akbar, "Your Majesty, you are absolutely right. I am a glutton. It is true that I have eaten a lot of dates. But Your Majesty, you really surprise me! How could you eat the dates along with the seeds?"

Birbal requested the courtiers to look under Akbar's chair. They did not see a single seed there. The courtiers could not control their laughter. Akbar was greatly embarrassed and could not hide his disappointment. Akbar had tried to play a trick on Birbal, but in the end, he himself became the butt of ridicule.

Akbar was embarrassed. But Birbal was his favourite. So he praised Birbal's wit and everybody was happy.

5. THE UNCONSCIOUS WITNESS

A Brahmin came to see the city of Delhi. He did not know anyone in the city. A merchant took pity on the Brahmin and gave him shelter. He also gave him some food to eat and a small room to sleep for the night.

There was a great menace of thieves in Delhi during those days. Emperor Akbar's guards patrolled the city streets during the nights. One of the guards himself was a thief. He used to steal things while he was on duty.

That night the guard came to the house of the merchant who had given shelter to the Brahmin. The Brahmin was fast asleep in a room. The guard made a hole in the wall and entered the room. In a corner of the room, he noticed a box belonging to the merchant. It was locked. The guard picked up the box and started to walk out of the room. Meanwhile, the Brahmin was awakened by the noise and the sound of the guard's footsteps. Seeing the Brahmin, the guard tried to escape. But the Brahmin caught him.

The guard tried to tempt the Brahmin. He said, "Please let me go. We will share the contents of this box equally between the two of us."

The Brahmin did not agree. He was about to shout for help and wake up the merchant. Suddenly, the guard started shouting. The merchant was awakened by the commotion. He arrived at the scene. Before the Brahmin could say a word, the guard said to the merchant, "Sir, this man was trying to run away with your box. I have caught him red-handed. Look sir, he has also made a hole in the wall."

The merchant believed the guard's story. Since the guard had caught the thief, the matter was taken to the court. The guard, the Brahmin and the merchant were produced before Birbal.

At first, Birbal called one of his trusted men and whispered something to him. The man left the court. Birbal called the guard and the Brahmin and started questioning them.

After some time, the man who had left the court came back running. He looked worried. He said to Birbal, "Sir, my son and I had gone to the Shiva temple. While we were coming out of the temple, my son fell down and became unconscious. I have to take him to a doctor. Sir, will you please send two of your men to help me?"

Birbal said, "Please wait here. I want you here for some important work. I will send this guard and the Brahmin to the temple. They will carry your son and bring him here. You need not worry."

The guard and the Brahmin reached the temple. They picked up the unconscious boy. While they were returning to the court, the Brahmin said to the guard, "Listen, brother! You were the one who broke into the merchant's house. You were running away with his box. I stopped you from stealing. Yet, you lied to everybody. Why did you trap me in this offence?"

The guard said, "You are right, but nothing can be done now. I had offered you half the share of the stolen things, but you did not agree. Now you will have to bear the punishment."

The guard and the Brahmin kept arguing with each other as they carried the boy to the court. When they reached the court, they laid the boy down on the floor.

Once again, Birbal asked the guard and the Brahmin to tell the truth. But each accused the other of the theft.

Birbal said, "Look, if both of you keep on arguing like this, how can I catch the thief?"

No sooner did Birbal say this than the 'unconscious' boy got up. He said to Birbal, "Sir, the guard is the real thief. He has trapped the poor Brahmin in this offence." The boy narrated the conversation between the guard and the Brahmin while they were bringing him to the court.

Birbal acquitted the Brahmin honourably and sent the guard to jail.

6. WHY IS THERE NO HAIR ON THE PALM?

One day, Akbar and Birbal went for horse riding. They rode on until they reached a small stream. Both were very tired. They dismounted from their horses and drank the cool and refreshing water of the stream. As Akbar was drinking water, he noticed deep marks of reins on his palms. He showed his palms to Birbal. Suddenly, Akbar had an idea. He asked, "Birbal, can you tell me why there is no hair on my palms?"

Birbal said, "Certainly, Your Majesty! Every day you generously give alms to the poor and the needy. And therefore, your palms get rubbed often. That is the reason why there is no hair on your palms."

Akbar was pleased with this explanation as it meant that he was very generous. But again, he said to Birbal, "I agree with what you say. But tell me Birbal, why is there no hair on your palms?"

Birbal said, "Your Majesty! You give me many gifts and rewards every day. My palms get rubbed when I receive them. So there is no hair on my palms, too."

Akbar said to himself, "What a clever fellow Birbal is!" But he still wanted to test Birbal by asking him a more difficult question. He said, "Birbal, I accept your explanation that our palms get rubbed several times during the day. But there is no hair on the palms of our courtiers, too. What reason have you to offer for that?"

Birbal smiled. He said, "Oh, yes! It is quite simple. You give me gifts and rewards every day. The courtiers do not appreciate this. They feel jealous and angry, but they are helpless. So they keep on rubbing their own palms. How can hair ever grow on palms which are always rubbed?" Hearing Birbal's reply, Akbar burst out laughing.

Akbar and Birbal then rode back to the palace.

7. THE GOLDEN GALLOWS

One day, when Akbar came to the court, he was furious. He spoke angrily to everybody. The courtiers could see that the Emperor was not in a good mood. They sat quietly till the Emperor left the court.

After Akbar went to his palace, Birbal asked him the reason for his anger. Akbar said, "Oh, forget it! It's my son-in-law. What a scoundrel he is! How can I control my anger?"

Birbal said, "Your Majesty, if you tell me what has happened, we can certainly find a solution to the problem."

Akbar said, "Birbal, it has been a year since I last saw my daughter. My son-in-law does not send her here to see me."

Birbal said, "Ah! That is not a problem at all! I will send somebody right away. He will go and bring Your Majesty's daughter here."

Akbar looked at Birbal and said, "I had already sent one of my trusted men. But my son-in-law is a stubborn man! He refuses to send my daughter to me. How I hate such sons-in-law! Birbal, can you do me a favour? Please arrange to put up gallows on the open ground in the city. I will send all the sons-in-law in my kingdom to the gallows."

Birbal was shocked. He tried to pacify Akbar. But Akbar was so furious that he refused to listen to Birbal. For the first time, Birbal was helpless. He had utterly failed to handle this situation. Disappointed, Birbal went to the city grounds and started making arrangements for the gallows.

After a couple of days, the gallows were ready. Birbal took Akbar to show him the gallows. Akbar was happy to see the gallows and he said, "Thank God. What a relief! Now I will eliminate all the sons-in-law in my kingdom."

Suddenly, Akbar noticed a golden gallows and a silver gallows. He asked Birbal, "For whom are these two special gallows?"

Birbal said, "The golden gallows is for you, Your Majesty. And the silver one is for me."

Akbar was in a quandary. He said to Birbal, "I did not ask you to do any such thing. Why should we go to the gallows?"

Birbal said, "Your Majesty, you wish to send all the sons-in-law in this kingdom to the gallows. Both of us are also the sons-in-law of somebody. How can we exclude ourselves when all the others are being sent to the gallows? Since you are the Emperor, I have arranged for a golden gallows for you. The silver one is for me, your most trusted man. How beautiful these two gallows look!"

Akbar was pleased with Birbal's wisdom. He realized his mistake and revoked his order.

8. THE PRINCE'S FRIEND

The Prince, Akbar's son, was friends with the son of one of the Emperor's commanders. The commander's son was an idler and a vagabond. But the Prince was very fond of him. He could not do without him and they were always seen together.

Akbar was worried that the Prince would be spoilt in the company of the commander's son. The Emperor did not wish his son to be influenced by the commander's son. At last, Akbar was so worried that he talked to Birbal about his problem.

One day, Birbal saw the Prince and the commander's son playing together in the garden. He went there and called the commander's son. When the boy came to him, Birbal pretended as if he was telling him something in his ear. He did not utter a word, but just stood there for some time. Fed up, the boy walked away.

As the boy was leaving, Birbal said loudly, "Please remember that whatever I have told you must be kept a secret. Do not disclose anything to anyone." The Prince, who was still around, heard this.

The boy came back to the Prince. The Prince asked him, "Friend, what did Birbal tell you?"

"Nothing," replied the boy.

The Prince said, "Look, you are my best friend. You will not keep any secrets from me, will you?"

The boy said, "Believe me, my friend. I am telling you the truth. Birbal did not tell me anything at all."

The Prince lost his temper and said, "I have seen both of you talking. Birbal surely said something in your ear. But it seems that you do not wish to tell me about it."

The boy was very angry with the Prince and went home. He thought, "I am sure the children of the rich are all alike. How suspicious they are! One should never befriend them."

The next day they did not even look at each other. Akbar was relieved.

But nobody ever came to know about the trick which Birbal had played to keep the two friends apart.

9. CALL HIM AT ONCE

Emperor Akbar woke up early one morning. Moving his fingers over his stubble he shouted, "Is anybody out there? Hurry up! Call him at once."

The attendant, waiting outside the room, was puzzled. Whom should he call? The Emperor had not asked for a particular person. He was too frightened to ask the Emperor to repeat his order.

The attendant asked another attendant for help. That attendant spoke to the third. The third attendant mentioned it to the fourth. In this way, all the attendants came to know about the Emperor's order. There was a commotion in the palace. Nobody knew whom the Emperor had called for.

Birbal was taking a stroll in the garden. He saw the attendants running here and there. He guessed that the Emperor must have issued some strange order. He called one of the attendants and asked him, "What is the problem? Why is everyone running around looking so worried and confused?"

The attendant told Birbal about the Emperor's order. He said, "His Majesty has not mentioned anyone in particular. Whom should we call? What should we do? If we fail to get someone soon, we will have to bear the brunt of his temper. Please help us, sir!"

Birbal said, "Tell me what the Emperor was doing when he gave the order."

The attendant thought for a while and said, "Well, nothing unusual. He was only moving his fingers over his stubble."

Birbal could guess what the order was. He said, "Take the barber to the Emperor immediately."

The attendant called the barber and took him to the Emperor. The Emperor thought, "How come the barber is here? I do not remember mentioning anyone in particular while giving out the order."

The Emperor asked the attendant, "Tell me the truth. Was it your own idea to call the barber or did someone help you?"

The attendant was nervous. He had no choice but to speak the truth. He said, "Your Majesty, it was Birbal's suggestion."

The Emperor was pleased with Birbal's wisdom.

10. OVERWISDOM

Emperor Akbar disliked flattery. Nobody ever dared to flatter him.

One day, it so happened that two courtiers were trying to gain the Emperor's favour by flattery. Finally, they said, "Your Majesty, trust us. We are ready to do whatever you wish. Please give us a chance to serve Your Majesty. We promise to do the tasks assigned to us in a matter of minutes."

Akbar knew very well that the two courtiers were only trying to flatter him. He decided to teach them a lesson. He said, "Actually, I cannot assign tasks to anyone just like that. But since both of you insist on it, I am asking each of you to do something for me."

"We are at your service, Your Majesty!" said the two courtiers.

Akbar said, "I want one of you to bring air in paper and the other to bring fire in paper."

Both the courtiers were dumbfounded. They said to themselves, "How strange and impossible these tasks are! We have invited trouble for ourselves!" Thinking thus, they left.

They spent many anxious days and sleepless nights pondering over the problem. They consulted the wise and referred to many books, too. But they could not find a way to complete the tasks assigned to them by the Emperor.

At last, they approached Birbal. They told him about their problem. They fell at Birbal's feet and said, "Only you can save us now, sir. We beg of you to help us."

Birbal took pity on the two courtiers. He said, "One of you should make a paper fan and the other should make a paper lantern. Take both the things to the Emperor. I am sure he will be pleased." The two courtiers thanked Birbal and left.

The following day, one of them made a paper fan and the other made a paper lantern and put a lighted candle in it. They took both the things to the court and placed them at the Emperor's feet.

Akbar was surprised to see the paper fan and the paper lantern. But he then remembered that he had ordered the two courtiers to bring air and fire in paper. He thought, "Ah! It is Birbal again! Only he can do such tasks so cleverly." The Emperor asked the two courtiers, "Tell me fellows, who gave you this idea? Tell me the truth or else be prepared for punishment."

The two courtiers trembled with fear. They said, "Your Majesty, if Birbal had not helped us, we would have failed to accomplish such difficult tasks."

Akbar pardoned both the courtiers after warning them strictly. He praised Birbal's wit and wisdom.

11. *PUNDIT'S* MOTHER TONGUE

Once a *pundit* came to the court of Emperor Akbar. Addressing the court, he said, "I challenge you to find out what my mother tongue is. If you fail to do so, you will have to accept defeat."

The courtiers asked the *pundit* many questions in different languages. But the *pundit* answered them in the language in which he was asked. He spoke all the languages as fluently as one speaks one's mother tongue. None of the courtiers could find out what the *pundit's* mother tongue was. Finally, he said to Akbar, "I give you seven days to find out my mother tongue. Do you accept the challenge?"

Akbar looked at Birbal. Birbal nodded in approval. Akbar said, "Yes. We accept your challenge."

The *pundit* was staying at an inn in the city. That night, when he was fast asleep, Birbal quietly entered his room. He tickled the *pundit's* ear with a blade of dry grass. The *pundit* was disturbed, but he went off to sleep again. Once again, Birbal tickled his ear. Now, the *pundit* was wide awake. He got up and shouted angrily in Gujarati, "Hey! Who is it? Why are you disturbing my sleep?"

He got down from his bed and looked around. Birbal was hiding himself in the room, but the *pundit* did not notice him. The *pundit* went back to sleep. Quietly, Birbal left the room and went home.

On the seventh day, the court assembled. The *pundit* was present there. Birbal spoke to the *pundit* in different languages. He said to Akbar, "Your Majesty, this *pundit's* mother tongue is Gujarati."

The *pundit* was astonished. He accepted defeat and left the court.

Akbar said, "Tell me, Birbal. How did you find out what the *pundit's* mother tongue was?"

Birbal said, "Very simple, Your Majesty! A man will speak his mother tongue either when he is in distress or when he is suddenly woken up from deep sleep." Birbal then told the court about his secret visit to the inn and explained how he had found out what the *pundit's* mother tongue was.

The courtiers admired Birbal for his wisdom. Akbar was so pleased that he rewarded Birbal with his most valuable necklace.

12. FOUR FOOLS

Akbar was a little whimsical. One evening, when he was going for a walk, he thought, "I do not have much work today. So, let me look out for at least four fools in my kingdom." He called Birbal and both of them set out in search of fools.

As they were walking, they came across a man riding a horse. There was a bundle of wood on his head. Birbal was surprised to see this sight. He asked the man, "Hey! Listen. Though you are riding a horse, why do you carry the load of wood on your head?"

The man replied, "Sir, this horse is very dear to me. He is already carrying my weight. So I am carrying this load of wood on my head. If I put it on him, it will be difficult for him to carry more weight!"

Birbal looked at Akbar and said, "Your Majesty, we have met the first fool."

Akbar said, "I agree. Now we have to look out for three more fools."

As they were still wandering in the streets, it became dark. So they started walking back to the palace. On their way back, they saw a man who was searching for something.

Birbal went up to him and asked, "Friend, what are you searching for?"

"I am searching for a coin which I lost here yesterday," said the man.

Birbal asked him, "But why are you searching for it today?"

The man replied, "I was very tired yesterday. So I have come to search for it today."

Birbal said, "Did you lose your coin exactly at this place?"

Pointing across the road, the man said, "No, not here. I lost it on that side."

Akbar was amazed. He said, "Hey! What sort of a man are you? You lost your coin on that side of the road and you are searching for it on this side!"

The man said, "Sir, it is very dark on that side. I cannot see anything there. Since there is some light here, it is easier to search here."

Akbar started laughing. Birbal said, "Your Majesty, this is the second fool."

They came back to the palace. Akbar said, "Birbal, we still have to look for two more fools. But that we will do tomorrow."

Birbal said, "Your Majesty, we no longer need to look out for them. Two fools are present right here."

Akbar said, "Here? What do you mean? Who are the two fools here?"

Birbal said, "Your Majesty, for no reason at all, I wasted my valuable time looking out for fools. Doesn't that prove that I am a fool, too?"

"And who is the fourth one?" asked Akbar.

Birbal said, "Pardon me, Your Majesty. For no reason at all, you accompanied me to look out for fools. Do you now realize who the fourth fool is?"

In his search for fools, Akbar proved himself to be a fool.

13. BIRBAL, THE COCK!

One day, Akbar decided to make fun of Birbal in order to embarrass him. He sought the help of his courtiers. He assembled them in the garden of his palace and said, "Last night I had a dream."

"Your Majesty, your dreams always come true," said one of the courtiers.

Akbar continued, "Well, I dreamt that anyone who would bring me an egg from the pond in my garden will be considered an honest and a pious man. The Almighty will always shower His blessings on him."

All the courtiers prepared themselves to jump into the pond. Akbar looked at Birbal and said, "Birbal, be prepared. Each of us will have to bring an egg from the pond."

But Birbal could not be fooled easily. He said, "Your Majesty, you should have the honour to jump into the pond first. The courtiers will follow you. I will be the last one to jump into the pond."

Akbar jumped into the pond and came out with an egg in his hand. The courtiers, too, jumped into the pond one after the other. Each one came out with an egg in his hand.

How could there be eggs in the pond? Actually, Akbar and his courtiers had planned everything beforehand. Each one of them jumped into the pond with an egg in his hand. When they came out, they would pretend as if they had found the egg in the pond.

At last, it was Birbal's turn. He jumped into the pond, but came out empty-handed. He stood before Akbar and crowed loudly, "Cock-a-doodle. ....doo." Akbar said, "Birbal, you could not get an egg from the pond. You are not an honest and a pious man. But why are you crowing?"

"Your Majesty! Only hens can lay eggs. I am a cock. How can I lay an egg?" said Birbal.

Birbal's reply implied that Akbar and the courtiers were all hens. This comment made them feel rather abashed.

14. THE MOST FAVOURITE

One day, Emperor Akbar was very angry with his wife for some reason. He said, "Begum! Go away to your father's house. Never show me your face again."

The Begum was worried and frightened. She went to Birbal to seek his help. She told Birbal about the Emperor's wrath and his order. Birbal asked her to do as he advised.

The Begum went back to the palace to meet the Emperor. When Akbar saw her, he turned his back on her. She said, "Your Majesty, I would not like to leave you. I wished to spend the rest of my life serving Your Majesty. But I will obey your order. Alas! I have no other choice now."

Without looking at his Begum, Akbar said, "Do not try to flatter me. Say whatever you want to say and leave quickly."

The Begum said, "Your Majesty, I am going to live in my father's house for the rest of my life. I wish to invite you to my palace for dinner tonight. And then, I request Your Majesty to allow me to take with me my most favourite thing. I will keep it with me as a remembrance of you."

That night, Akbar went to his Begum's palace for dinner. The Begum served him his favourite dishes. At the end of the dinner, she also offered him a *paan*. The Begum had secretly added a sleeping pill in his *paan*. As soon as Akbar chewed the *paan*, he lay on the bed and was fast asleep. The Begum sent for Birbal.

Birbal came with a carriage. He carried Akbar, put him in the carriage and sent him to the house of the Begum's father. The Begum also went along with him.

The following morning, when Akbar opened his eyes, he looked around. He found himself in an unfamiliar place. Suddenly, he saw his Begum sitting near the bed. Before Akbar could say a word, the Begum said, "Pardon me, Your Majesty! Do you remember? You had granted me the permission to take with me my most favourite thing. How could anything in this world be more precious than Your Majesty? You are, indeed, my most favourite. So, I have brought you here along with me."

Akbar was glad to hear his Begum's words. He realized his mistake and returned to his palace along with his Begum.